CHAPTER ONE   **A CHANGE O.**

"Maw!! Whit's fir breakfast?"

"Yer big enough and ugly enough to make it yersel', I'm away to work."

My name is Jamie Johnson, my pals call me JJ. I'm 27 and I still stay wi' ma wee Maw. Her name's Terry and she works in the local textiles factory where she's worked for 32 years. I'm unemployed; I live in the arse end of naewhere and I'm fucking skinto. I used to work with my Maw in that same fucking textiles factory, but when they paid me on a Thursday they never fucking seen me again tae the Monday. Bookies, pub and shagging. That was me from a Thursday right through to the Monday morning. My life had to change. I needed that wee bit of luck and I also needed to get oot of this shitey wee toon.

"A'right JJ, whit can a get ye pal?"

"A Racing Post and a can of Irn Bru, Sammy."

"A Racing Post haha? Gie' it up man. Aw your fucking horses end up on Blackpool beach for 50 pence a shot ya daftie."

"Aye well you'll see Sammy. I woke up this morning wi' a different mindset. I'm gonnae fucking be somebody man and get oot of this toon. You'll see."

"Yeah, yeah JJ."

Fucking prick that Sammy. Always fucking bamming me up man. I'll show him.

The local bookie's was always thriving. You had Tam, the Manager, who hated paying you a penny. It was like it was his ain fucking money he was gie'in you. The lassies that worked there were a'right. Four in total, on two separate shifts. Tina, Laura, Megan and Paige. The punters were a'right too and every noo and then you'd get the odd tip from some cunt and you'd manage to get a few pints afore ye went up the road. I had £18.11 and if I managed to double that I'd be happy, go to the pub, get a few pints, then head hame so my Maw could make my dinner.

The Challenge was on!!

Now, I need to make things clear here. No matter what time you go into the bookies, one punter was always in there. Hugo!! Now, Hugo was my type of guy, a decent guy. He never drank, swore like fuck and must've flung a lifetime's supply of bookie pens at the big telly for all his losers. He wasn't long out the jail, being the local drug dealer. Being the local drug dealer meant one thing as well though, Hugo had plenty of readdies. He was always a'right with me and if I needed dough, Hugo would slip me some and I would give him it back when I could. He was on a Tag and had to be in from 9pm to 9am. The racing was normally finished at these times anyway so it suited Hugo down to the ground.

"JJ my boy"!! "How are you getting on son?"

"Aye, no bad Hugo."

"Much ye punting wi' the day son?"

"Well I've got close tae a score on me so double that will dae me the day. Ye got any tips, Hugo?"

"Well aye, a dae. I really fancy 'A Class Above' in the next at Ascot. 4/1 shot JJ, get yer hoose on it son."

"My hoose? My fucking Wendy hoose, aye?"

Hugo's gave me this tip, I need to go for it. Hugo brings about £3000 in to the bookies every day. Nae cunt says a word to him 'cause he's basically laundering his drug money through the local bookies. Tam the Manager knows he's dain it, the four lassies know he's dain it and so does the whole fucking toon. The problem is, every cunt likes Hugo. If he was a dick, some cunt would grass him in but like I said, he's a guid guy.

My £18.11 soon whittles doon to £10. I've frittered the £8.11 on fucking virtual horses, greyhounds and horses running in South Africa fur fucks sake. I'm a dick. Every fucking two minutes there's something else to bet on. I'd bet on two fucking ants running along the ground.

So, finally, it's here. The 2.25 at Ascot. I run over to the desk, confident as fuck.

"£10 on A Class Above please Tam, to win my good man. Oh, and

I'll take the 4/1 price on that too please, Sir."

Tam's looking at me as if to say, "..you won't see that ten pounds ever again son..."

4/1 soon becomes 2/1. Every man and his dug is on the horse. Surely it must win?

And..... We're off!! Hugo's going Kate fucking Bush at the telly as usual.

"C'mon you, ya cunt. Fucking go, go, go."

His pen is poised to hit the plastic sheet covering the glass on the 60 inch monitor. A Class Above fucking hoses in.

"Ya fucking beauty"!!

Tam's raging haha. Paige, who's working wi' Tam the day, geez me a wee wink cause she thinks it's hilarious as well if he has to pay oot.

I approach the desk.

"Tam, can I ermmm, cash this in please, Sir?"

"Erm, I'm busy JJ, can you get Paige to do it son?"

Hahahaha. The cunt is bealin'. Paige pays me my £50, I high five Hugo then see the next race. I've got £50 in my hawn, but the next favourite is an evens money shot. I completely convince masel' it's gonnae win. Hugo's telling me to go to the pub and enjoy my winnings. I'm thinking, £50 in my wallet or £100 in my wallet? It's a no brainer here. I put the £50 on the favourite to win and assume the position.

I huv to tell you about Donald. Donald comes in to the bookies to annoy every cunt. I've never seen him put a bet on in my life but he likes to tell ye about all his winners from the previous day. He says he puts his bets on at the only other bookies in the toon but comes in to oors 'cause it's a better atmosphere and telly. The guy annoys the fucking life oot me. So, the race starts, I've got Donald in my lug.

"Whit wan you oan here son?"

"The favourite, Donald."

"Oh it's no gawn too well, son."

I can feel the rage already building.

"Oh that was a bad jump son."

I wish this cunt would just fuck off. Pumped!! A 16/1 shot wins and only Donald would come away with this one.

"Oh aye, my brother telt me about that 16/1 shot this morning, I think I put 50p on it tae win."

The CUNT!! This is the kind of pish he comes away wi'. Hugo's flung about four pens at the telly; I storms oot the bookies.

"Bye JJ," says Tam. I'm fucking raging.

Why did I no' just go to the pub with the £50? I'm thinking £50 or £100 pound? I'm no' fucking thinking zero pounds am I? Dick!! Racing Post gets flung in the bin and I toddle up the road.

When is my luck going to change man? I'm stuck in a rut. Nae joab, nae bird, nae money and nae fucking luck. I need a change of fortune - and soonish.

CHAPTER TWO   NICE BUNNET

A few days pass and finally my Giro money is in my account. My direct debits come oot the morra, so I'm gonna just lift it aw. Hopefully win and put the money back in my account so I don't miss the debits. I always use the cash machine ootside Sammy's store. I withdraw the full £140. That's two weeks money. I bounce straight in to Sammy's.

"A Racing Post and a can of Irn Bru please Samuel."

"Samuel, eh? Somebody's in a gid mood. Get a ride last night JJ?"

"Jist yer wife, Sammy. Prick."

Straight to the bookies. I opens the door.

"Morning Tam, morning Megan and good morning Hugo."

I chew the fat with Hugo and write down the horses he fancies and the ones I like for the day. I decide to change tack for today and head to the pub for a pint before I go back to the bookies.

Now in Scotland, if you're over 50, it's pretty much socially acceptable that you wear a bunnet. Any working class person's pub in Scotland will show this. As soon as you fling the doors open, you're seeing at least four to ten guys in there with bunnets oan. I've never wore one myself because at only 27, I'd probably get my cunt kicked in.

A wee Irish guy with a bunnet on starts talking to me.

"Hello son, I see you've got a Racing Post there, fancy anyting today?"

"Aye a couple Sir."

I gets my wee list oot that myself and Hugo had compiled and give the wee guy a look.

"Tell me now, why don't you have a bunnet on boy? You're the only langer in here that isn't wearing one."

Basically whit he means is, it's full of auld cunts and aw the boys my age are at work.

"Ermmm, I've never wore wan mate."

"You've never wore one? How do you think we can all afford to drink every day?"

I'm looking at this auld codger completely confused now.

"Well my friend, let me give you a wee tip. Wearing a bunnet helps you concentrate more and it keeps the light out of your eyes so there's no distractions when you're in the bookies. No distractions mean more winners."

There's eight auld guys in this pub, I look roon. They've all got half a lager and a whisky sitting beside them. The auld bastards are in here aw day, every day. The auld yin is right. A bunnet it is!!

I toddles doon to the local Charity shop. Opens the door and makes my way inside. Now, I've never been in a Charity shop before but it smelt like some cunt had poured a can of Kestrel on the carpet; took a shite on it and shut the doors and windaes through an Indian Summer. The place was fucking honking. Needs must JJ, needs must. The wee wummin behind the counter asked if she could help me.

"Aye, eh, I'm looking fir wan of they auld man's bunnets."

She directs me to the four in the shop. I tries the four of them on, now the cunts that owned these hats must've hud a heed like a fucking Aberdeen Angus. There's no way any of the four of them were fitting me.

Betty from the Charity shop told me that was all they had in stock. My Maw's pal, Janice, volunteers in the charity shop as well and after trying on the four bunnets, I hear the bell go as somebody had walked in. It was Janice who was carrying a broon box.

"A'right JJ, wit you dain in here?"

"I'm looking fir a bunnet, Janice, but aw these wans would be too big for the Elephant Man." "Well, we've just had this box donated from the late Father Jackson's estate."

Father Jackson was the local priest. When I say was, aye, he just died a week ago. He was Irish and absolutely hilarious. He never joined the priesthood until he was 40 something, but what a legend he was. The stories he told at Mass about a multi-millionaire friend of his, before he joined the priesthood, were unbelievable.

Janice tipped his box on to the big table and sure as shit, there was a bunnet. A wee brown thing with a wee four leaf clover embroidered on the side of it. I put it on my heed and it fitted absolutely perfectly.

"I'll take it."

I paid for my new bunnet and made my way back to the bookies. This was gonnae be it. I hud a pint in me, a pep talk from the auld yin and a new bunnet. Nothing could stop me now.

I swung the doors open of the bookies. The usual suspects were in. I got Laura to make me a coffee then I sat in my usual seat, next to Hugo, to get ready for the day ahead.

"Nice bunnet son", said Hugo.

He gave me a wink, laughed, then we both got our game faces on. Tam and the bookies were taking one almighty beating today. I could feel it in my water.

CHAPTER THREE   THE TIDE IS TURNING

Wan thing aboot our local bookies was, it was either two temperatures. Roasting, or fucking Baltic. Now, Scotland isn't exactly the Costa Del Sol - so why we have fucking air con in the first place is beyond me. It's cause that miserable bastard Tam doesn't want the door left open I bet. I've got my list of tips, I've got the good Faither's bunnet on and I'm feeling good. I've got £130 on me 'cause my Racing Post, my Irn Bru and my Bunnet cost me a tenner aw in. Here we fucking go!!

The start is sensational. The first 3 winners are in. The auld Irish cunt in the pub was spot on. Nothing is distracting me with my Bunnet on. No' even that cunt Donald.

"Oh nice Bunnet JJ, where did you get that?" he said.

"Harrods ya prick now beat it."

Hugo bursts oot laughing.

"Aw, nae wunner Hugo, he does my fucking Brad Pitts in man."

Hugo chuckles away at my reply to auld Donald. The auld yin gets the message, stays away from me and goes and bugs somebody else.

I've had three winners in a row. Surely something has to go wrong at some point? Me and Hugo are firing through our secretive wee list and sure as shit, we're getting winner after winner. Unbelievable!! I can see Donald looking over, he's wondering why me and Hugo are constantly high fiving each other and picking winner after winner. He'll be raging the auld cunt.

Donald disappears and then turns up with his brother, Pedro and Davie the mulkman. He's obviously telt them about our wee turn of fortune and has brought them in to try and get a piece of our lucky turn. Now as I mentioned earlier, the bookies is either roasting or fucking Baltic. With my Bunnet and trackie tap on and with about fifteen folk in the bookies now, it was fucking roasting. There were four more horses still on our list, I had nearly £500 in my pocket and was hoping to walk out of there with at least a Grand now.

I takes the Bunnet aff and I look like I've just dipped my heid in the chip pan. Fucking sweat is lashing aff me. I place the Bunnet on tap of my trackie tap in the corner of the bookies and write down my next bet. Hugo suggests we just do a Lucky 15 instead with the last four horses as we canny seem to lose. I don't want to risk all of my £500, so I put £150 on my Lucky 15 and Hugo follows suit. That's 15 bets at £10 each for our four remaining horses. We sit back, smug as fuck, hoping that the four sail home.

"CUNT!!"

After the 4th race, Hugo is going absolutely Kate Bush at the telly. I counted four wee blue pens hitting the telly like machine gun fire. Not one of our four horses won. Pish!! Ah well, we had a good turn the day. I put my trackie tap and my Bunnet oan and head oot the door. I head to the bank with £350. I put the money in the bank to cover my direct debits and have a wee bit extra gambling money for the morra. I think I'll buy my wee Maw a Chinese the night. A guid day.

CHAPTER FOUR   THE WEE IRISH GUY

Another dollar, another day. Up and at 'em JJ. I woke up to the smell of Chinese food reeking the fucking hoose oot. I bought that much Chinese food last night for me and Maw that I couldn't shut the bin right wi' aw the plastic containers hinging oot it. The hoose was fucking honking man.

I was feeling guid the day. A good £220 profit yesterday. All my direct debits taken care of and a full belly for my wee Maw. It gets her aff my case about getting a job for a few days anaw. Everything was taken care of except the wee Irish guy who gave me the advice aboot 'the Bunnet', so I head doon to the pub to buy the auld cunt a pint or two.

I mince into the Battle Cruiser and there's nae cunt in, barring Davie the mulkman. He works through the night, so being in the pub at 10am isn't such a bad thing for him. Mel, behind the bar starts pouring my usual pint of Tennents and after giving Davie a wee nod, I sit at the end of the bar.

> "Will you take that fucking bunnet aff ya eeijit?" says Davie. "Yer in yer 20's son, yer no 60 odd fur fuck sake."

> "Aye, aye Davie, drink yer pint ya belter. I'll take the bunnet aff, when you take 3 staine aff ya fat tcunt."

Mel chuckles away at the ensuing banter and it's not long before the regulars start pouring in to join in with the craic. Prick this and prick that. Cunt this and cunt that. If a tourist walked in, they'd think World War 3 was about to start but that's just how folk from the West Coast of Scotland are. We don't mix our words and we don't suffer fools gladly.

"Mel!!

"Another Tennents, JJ?"

"Naw, I'm a'right the noo hen. I was in here yesterday talking to a wee Irish guy. Have you seen him aboot the day?"

"Naw JJ, he was only over for Father Jackson's funeral. He's away back to Ireland on this morning's boat."

"Ah fur fuck's sake man."

"Wits rang wi ye JJ?"

"Och he gave me a wee bit of advice and I just wanted to buy him a couple of pints."

"Wit was the advice, take that bunnet aff cause ye look like a tadger?" said Davie the mulkman. "Piss aff you!! Naw, it was more meaningful, spiritual advice if you like. No' that you'd know anyway ya dafty."

Mel started telling me what the auld Irish guy got up to when I left the pub yesterday.

"Once you left, he started to tell me a wee bit about himself and how he was Faither Jackson's best pal. They went to Primary school the gither and did pretty much everything together. He put £500 behind the bar and everybody had a right good day on the auld yin. He said his name was James and how he grew up in a wee town West of Cork called, 'Ballincollig', with Father Jackson. He said they were wild when they were younger and he couldn't believe that 'Pete' joined the priesthood."

I finished my pint and left the pub. I was gutted that I never got to catch up wi' the wee Irish guy to get him a couple of pints, tell him about my winnings and see if he had any more good advice. It's mental that he knew Father Jackson. I wish he'd said he was over for his funeral. Ah well, what's meant to be is meant to be in life. I guess I wisnae supposed to see the auld codger again.

Maybe I'll surprise the auld yin wan day. If my mini streak continues then mibee I'll head over to Ballin whatever the fuck it was called and surprise auld James and thank him for his advice aboot the Bunnet. At least it got me a couple of winners yesterday and kept that cunt Donald oot my peripheral vision. Let's see what today brings!!

›

I toddle in to the bookies, still kinda pissed aff I missed auld Irish James. Not to worry, I had auld Scottish Tam staring right at me as soon as I swung the door open.

"Morning, JJ !!"

"Morning, Tam."

"I hear you and Hugo gave us a skelping yesterday, from Laura?"

"We did that Thomas. Expect more the day, ya auld walloper. Morning, Hugo."

"Morning, JJ."

One thing I never told ya about Hugo. See when he's reading the Racing Post, he doesn't wear his glasses like any other cunt. They're right on the end of his beak. He's scouring away and we go over today's battle plan.

Alberto, the Italian guy minces in. Alberto is a cracking wee guy. He works at the local tip and if you need a horse to pull you oot the shit, Berto is normally the man to go to. He's a quiet guy and, like me, canny stand Donald. The one thing I love about him as well is that he never gets involved in the banter in the bookies, but likes to fling a wee lure in every now and again. Then he walks away and waits for some cunt to bite - haha. Usually it's Donald.

The bookies is like fucking Greenland. Tam turns the air-con up to fucking annoy me I'm sure of it. Bunnet and jaicket on the day. The cunt won't beat me, I'm prepared for the fucking South Pole man. I've even brought gloves and a scarf the day. Prick.

I took a hunner pound oot the cashline this morning. If I lose it, I lose it. I'm going all out today. Big price winners, is the plan. I can feel it in my water for sure.

Hugo compiles his list - and I compile mine. Hugo's got his usual £3000 and I've got my hunner bucks. We cross check each other's list. We've only got one horse the same, oddly enough. Electric Eleanor in the 4.10 at Sandown, at 20/1. Hugo decides to go with his list and I decide to go with mine.

My List

12.30	Lingfield	Duncan the Drunk		10/1
12.50	Ayr	Fat Tony	14/1	
13.25	Sandown	LA Linea		33/1
14.30	Lingfield	Comatose Kay		12/1
14.50	Ayr	Gibraltar Sun		40/1
16.10	Sandown	Electric Eleanor		20/1

We're four races in on my list and all I can hear is...

"Whit's fucking happening here?!!"

Hugo is going Kate Bush at the telly. None of his first four horses have came in and my first four have, unbelievably, won. A 10/1, 14/1, 33/1 and a 12/1 shot. I cannae fucking believe it. My pocket is already bulging and my 40/1 shot is up next. Hugo has had to run across the road to his hoose for mare money. His three grand is gone. He's fucking seething, but Tam is grinning like a Cheshire cat behind the counter.

Hugo gets back just in time for the 14.50, at Ayr. He says that ma donkey has fucking no chance at 40's and backs the 11/4 favourite. £2000 on it to win. A madman - haha. He's chasing his losses now. I just play it safe, twenty pound on Gibraltar Sun at 40's.

"The favourite, Clarence The Gangster and Gibraltar Sun are neck and neck with 100 yards to go!! They're still neck and neck with 50 yards to go!!.."

Hugo is going fucking mental. Mental chicken oriental.

"MON YAAAAAA CUNT!!!"

They go over the line together. Photo Finish!!

The next two minutes are tense. Hugo is pacing up and doon like a madman ready to explode. I'm kinda hoping his wins noo 'cause ma pockets are full. Tam is watching, on hoping he loses.

"Result from the 14.50 at Ayr. First, number 4 Gibraltar Sun!!"#

Hugo hits the fucking roof.

Hugo storms oot the bookies. He's flung about 50 pens rapid at the telly. He's five grand doon, I'm going up to the counter to collect £820.

Tam says, "Would you just like that in those 50's that Hugo just gave me?"

"Cunt!!"

Hugo texts me to say that he was finished for the day. I said for him to head back over for that last wan on our list. He said he'll see. I go into the toilets to count ma money. £2220. I cannae believe it, I've never had so much money in my life. I ran to the bank and put £2000 into my account, head for a couple of pints and then back to the bookies for my last horse of the day.

I get to the bookies ten minutes before the race. With my luck the day I think, 'feck it'. I spent £20 in the pub, so I've got £200 left.

"£200 on Electric Eleanor to win please, Thomas."

"Right son, you just don't know when to leave it, dae ye? You've won a fortune the day, but one last bet, eh?"

"I'll take the 20/1 thanks, Tam."

As Tam puts the money in the till, I see all of poor Hugo's crisp £50 notes.

They're talking about the race now and my horse doesn't even get a mention. It goes from 20/1 out to 25/1. I'm thinking that my luck is about to run out. It goes to an advert, two minutes until the race starts. The doors swing open and in walks Hugo.

"Evening Tam."

"Ah, back again Hugo?"

"Aye, Tam, £500 each way on Electric Eleanor please."

"Are you taking the 25's Hugo?"

"Aye, Tam, aye."

Hugo takes his seat, looks at me and nods.

"I'm sorry if I've fucked ye here JJ. I've hud nae luck the day whatsoever, son."

"Och, don't worry aboot it Hugo, man. You'll get it back mate."

The race begins!! Electric Eleanor starts off terribly. I can see Tam smiling out of the corner of my eye. Hugo has put £6000 in the cunt's till the day - and he's loving every single second of this. Two furlongs to go, with a fence to jump. The loose horse takes out the favourite at the last, who was 10 lengths clear and Electric Eleanor eases down at the finish for a comprehensive victory.

"Ya FUCKING beauty"!!

Me and Hugo are fucking dancing!! I fling my Bunnet aff the roof. Donald starts to walk oot the bookies.

Alberto says, "Yer brother no gie ye a tip for that Donald, ya dick?"

Outstanding fae the wee Italian. Tam is raging!! Tina and Paige are giving us the thumbs up from behind the counter. What a day!!

£4200 to me for £200 to win, at 20/1 and more importantly for me today - £16,625 for his £500 each way bet at 25's, for Hugo. Tam is fucking beeling. He has enough to pay me mine but Hugo's has to go on his card Tam says.

Hugo says, "No, I don't want it on my card, I'd like cash please, sir."

Hugo knows fine well that Tam has to go to the bank and get every single penny in cash.

I wait around until Tam gets back and he grimaces as he counts all of Hugo's money out. It was fucking brilliant to watch. The bank shuts at five o'clock, so I need to get oot of here pronto and get this money banked. I shake Hugo's hand, say goodnight to Tam, Tina and Paige and grab my trusted Bunnet aff the floor and head doon the High Street. Six winners out of six - and six grand up for the day - I cannae quite believe it.

Off to the Bank and then off to the pub to celebrate!!

CHAPTER SIX   **WHERE'S MY BUNNET?**

"Where the fuck am I?"

Urghhhhhh. I can hear snoring behind me. Aw, fur fuck sake. Who did I pump last night? If I turn roon and it's a guy, a murder will be committed in this room.

Here goes......

Aw, fur fuck sake it's Bonnie!! Bonnie is the local bike. We in Scotland like to call lassies like Bonnie a 'Ten to 2' burd. Basically, if you cannae get a ride, then you buy Bonnie a drink about ten minutes to 2am and yer sorted. A definite ride. To be fair, she's a nice enough lassie but she just loves the boaby. She's had a shot at the title from me a few times now, but all other options have been exhausted or like last night by the looks of things, I've sank about 20 pints.

"Bonnie!! Bonnie!! Wake up fur fuck sake."

"Och, whit man?"

"Where the fuck did I meet you last night?"

"Can you no' remember ya drunken arsehole, naw?"

"Obviously no', or I widnae be asking ye, would I?"

"I walked into the pub aboot 10pm and you were well gone by then. Ye were buying everybody in the pub drink, saying you and Hugo got a guid turn on the horses. Tina and Paige from the bookie's were in. Donald, his brother and Davie the mulkman were in too, with a few locals. You were on top form that's for sure. Ye were up dancing, buying Champagne and Whisky for everybody. You were Mr.Popular!! We got a kebab, a taxi and then came back here. Don't worry, nothing happened, ye were blitzed. I just wanted to make sure you were a'right, pal."

"Och, cheers pal. I really appreciate it, Bonnie. Can I take you oot for breakfast to thank ye?"

"Naw yer alright pal, I'm knackered so I'm going back to sleep."

"Ok, pal. Well, I better shoot doon the road. Cheers for looking after me, I owe you wan."

I'm kinda glad she said naw, in a way. Cunts would start ripping intae me if they seen me out wi' her. They'd think she was my burd or something. You know that way? I start gathering my things. Jeans, T-Shirt, skants, socks, trainers. I'm fucking missing something here......

My Bunnet!!

"Bonnie, have you seen my Bunnet, pal?"

"Yer Bunnet? Whit Bunnet?"

"I had a Bunnet oan last night."

"No' when you got here ye never, 'cause I undressed ye."

"Aw no way man, I kinda liked that wee hing. I'll phone the taxi company and see if it got handed in... Hello, can I get a taxi from 8 Smith Drive, heading to 69 Charles Street, please? Oh, and while yer oan, a broon Bunnet, with a four leaf clover embroidered on it never got handed in did it?"

"Naw, son, nothing."

"Okidoki, nae bother. I'll try the Kebab shop later, Bonnie. Laters."

Right so Kebab shop or pub? It has to be in wan eh them.

"Wit number at Charles Street, son?"

"69, Mr."

The driver draps me aff. I get in the hoose; showered, brush the teeth, get changed and head doon to the kebab shoap. The fucking place is shut. Doesn't open until 5pm. Ah well, I'll pop into the pub and see if it's there. Mel's probably got it behind the bar for me.

I'm walking towards the pub and I've got the fucking fear. The "fear" in Scotland is when you wake up in the morning after getting pished and you canny remember whit the fuck ye got up tae the night before. I've definitely got the fear. Is Mel going to boot my baws here, or whit?

"JJ"!! Here he is!! Mr.Moneybags himself. I was thinking about staying closed the day with the amount of money you put in ma till last night. Tennents?"

"Eh, aye Mel cheers."

"Ye were on top form last night JJ."

"Eh, aye, so I've been hearing. Ye huvnae seen my Bunnet have ye, Mel? Cannae mind what I done wi' it, but I definitely came in here wi' it."

"Naw pal, definitely no' here. Gimme five minutes and we'll fast forward through the CCTV to see if we can spot it."

Mel gets the remote control oot for the CCTV telly.

"Wit time did ye come in?"

"Aboot hawf five, Mel."

5.37pm. Sure as shit, I come walking into the pub - Bunnet on heid. All the folk Bonnie mentioned were in. As it starts going through the hours.

"Stoap, stoap, stoap!!"

Mel stoaps the DVD. I'm up dancing wi' Tina and she takes my Bunnet aff my heed and puts it on hers. Ye know when wan fucker steals yer hat, the whole pub needs a shot? Aye, well that's what happened. It started getting passed round everybody.

"Donald!! That cunt is the last to wear it. See?"

Donald walks oot the pub at 7.25pm with ma Bunnet oan and doesn't appear back all night.

"Have you got his number, Mel?"

"Naw JJ, I huvnae son."

"Och, I'll see the cunt later on in the bookies."

I have another couple of pints, then walk across the road to the bookies.

"Tam, you seen Donald this efternoon?"

"Naw JJ and probably won't see him fir aboot a month either."

"How's that?"

"He was waiting for me opening this morning. He won a substantial amount on a Fitba' accumulator last night. I obviously cannae say how much, but it was a lot of cash."

"Eh? That cunt never wins. We'll never hear the fucking end of this noo, Hugo."

Hugo just shakes his heid.

"Have you got his number Tam? He's got my Bunnet."

"I wondered where he'd got that fae. Aye, he came in here last night with wan oan and I asked him where he got it. He said you were across the road steaming and everybody in the pub had a shot of it. So he was just keeping it safe for you and was gonna give you it the day when he seen ye in case ye loast it."

"Ah right, it all makes sense now. Here's me thinking he's an auld prick and the auld codger has looked after my Bunnet fir me. Maybe he's no' a prick efter all. He probably only won cause he had my wee Bunnet on. This'll be fun when he walks in now. He'll be gloating about his win for years. I wonder if his brother gave him all the Fitba' teams?

I run over tae the cashpoint and take out £300 to play with. Less than hour later it's all gone. I go to the bank and take out another £500 to try and get my £300 back. Less than an hour later, £800 gone, in total.

"Fuuuuuuuuck"!!

Back tae the Pub.

I'm in the pub ten minutes and the door swings open, it's Donald.

"JJ son, missing something?"

"Aye, £800 and a Bunnet."

"I've got your Bunnet, son. I took it hame last night in case you lost it wee man, ye were steaming. Sorry I haven't been in earlier, I've been away ordering a new bathroom, a new fridge freezer, a new washing machine and a new dryer."

"Ye won the lottery Donald?"

"No' far aff it, son. I won £8237 last night on a Fitba' accumulator, 16 teams."

"Well done you."

"Here's yer Bunnet, son, I need to shoot."

"Cheers, Donald."

Ah well, at least the auld yin got a gutid turn and done the sensible thing. Bought stuff fir his hoose and never gave it back to the bookies. I'm £800 doon the day and I'm just topping myself up wi' the drink from last night. I better get up the road. I've made a right cunt of it the day but, hey, at least I got my wee Bunnet back.

"Night, Mel!!"

"Night, JJ!!"

Losing the £800 the other day - and Donald winning over £8000 - kinda scunnered me. I've stayed oot the pub and oot the bookie's. Hugo always says to me that after a big loss, you should regroup and come back a few days later and go again. So that's what I did. Back to my auld routine cause I was getting a bit cocky there.

"A Racing Post and a bottle of Irn Bru please, Sammy."

"Whit's this auld Donald has been showing you and Hugo how it's done in that bookies JJ?"

"Piss aff Sammy, it's the first time he's ever won anything."

"I heard you've no' been in a couple of days and noo he's in your seat next to Hugo?"

"You better be fucking winding me up, Sammy."

"I'm no', JJ."

Noo I've got my Bunnet back fae Donald, naebody is gonnae distract me today. It's firmly attached to my Cranium. Racing Post is in my hawn and I've tanned a bottle of Irn Bru. I'm good to go. I burst into the bookies. Nae sign of Donald on my chair, but the usual suspects are in.

"Hugo, whit's this Donald has been sitting in my chair?"

"Naw, JJ he huznae."

"That cunt Sammy bamming me up again, the prick."

"Eh?"

"Aw, nothing Hugo."

"Ye done yer list, JJ?"

"No' yet, Hugo. Give me ten minutes to have a wee study, eh?"

It's fucking minus 70 in the bookies again so everything is on again today, barring my gloves and scarf.

"Fucking Baltic in here, Tam."

"Och shut yer hole, JJ. It's only you that's cauld. Dick."

My magic touch is back. Everything I'm backing is winning. This could be another massive day. Because it's freezing, I'm drinking coffee like it's going out of fashion. So excuse the pun, but I'm pishing like a racehorse.

I'm standing pishing away with a big smile on my face. My pockets are full again. I'm winning race after race. Shall I just finish this pish and head to the pub? I've won enough. I might lose it all. Ah, one more bet, fuck it. The auld Irish guy was right last week. I do concentrate more with the Bunnet on. I never had it on the other day and lost £800. He's right, the old guy was right.

Hey, wait a fucking minute here. I've had this oan since I got in and won every, single, bet. Donald had it oan the other day and won his first ever bet that we all ken aboot. The day before that, I won a fortune. Did I have the Bunnet oan? Aye, I fucking did!! Right, when I got back oot there, I'm trying something.

"Oaft!! You turned that heating up, Tam? Fucking roasting in here, man."

I casually slip the Bunnet and the jaiket aff. It's only about minus 60 now. I put three bets on for the next three races. Yup, sure as shit, all three lose. I casually slips the Bunnet on, and put £50 on a 12/1 shot, dug in trap 6. Basically, I could beat this fucking thing. Trap 6 hoses up.

I cannae fucking believe this. Alberto is in and has lost a few races now. I give him the speech about the Bunnet that the old Irish guy gave me. I tell him about how it makes you concentrate and that. I tell him that the Charity shop have a couple in and to take a shot of mine to see if it helps him. I sit back and watch as he wins the next two races. He gives me my Bunnet back and runs over to the Charity shop.

I look around to see if anybody has clicked. I have a lucky Bunnet. As long as it's on yer napper, you cannae lose. A no lose Bunnet!!

What do I do? Do I tell anybody? Surely I have to tell Hugo? Naw, I cannae. What if it breaks the streak? My luck will run out. What can I do? Who can I tell? Oh, I need a pint man - and fast - while I think about this. Maybe Mel will be able to give me some advice. I need to talk to somebody and fast.

I sit doon in the corner of the pub with my pint. My fucking mind is going into overdrive here, man. What will I fucking do? I've got money in the bank. I need to get away fae here. I'll take my Bunnet, go to Vegas and make an absolute fortune. Naw, naw. Aw, think JJ. If it wisnae for that auld I Irish guy in here, telling me to buy this fucking thing, then I wouldn't be sitting here stressing out like this.

That's it!! I'll go and visit the auld Irish guy and see if he has any advice on what to do.

"Mel!!

"Another pint already, JJ?"

"Naw, naw, Mel. Mind I was in last week asking about that auld Irish guy that was over for the Faither's funeral?"

"Aye, whit aboot him?"

"Where did he say he was from again? Whit was the name of the place?"

"Ermmmm, Ballinsomething, wasn't it?"

"Aye that was it."

"Google it, JJ. It was West of Cork, I remember that."

I get my phone out for a Map of Ireland and look West of Cork and yes, there it is.

"Ballincollig it was, Mel. Ya beauty !!"

"Whit dae ye want to know that for, ya dafty?"

"I think I'm going to pay the auld guy a visit. He seemed like a nice auld fella. He was good to talk to and gave me some good advice.

I think I'll pop over for a couple of days and take the auld yin oot for a few pints."

"Where are you getting all the money fae lately, JJ? I thought you were skint and plus you don't work?"

"Eh, I got lucky the other day on the horses mind?"

Mel goes back to serving pints. Too many questions there for my liking, I cannae let anybody get suspicious about my Bunnet. It would get nicked in seconds if anybody fun oot. I need to book a flight to Cork, sharpish, and try and get to this wee toon to find auld James - and fast.

I head up the road. Get my maws laptop oot and book a flight to Cork for the following morning and a B&B in Ballincollig, as it doesn't have any Hotels. I'm heading into the unknown here, but I need to get out of here for a few days and get some advice aff the auld codger before anybody finds oot aboot my Bunnet.

I don't know what I'm heading into here and I don't know if telling James is the right thing to do. It was his advice that got me here in the first place. I hope he can give me the advice to do what's best for me, my wee Maw and the rest of my wee toon. If anybody in my toon finds oot about this Bunnet, then all hell could break loose. I leave my wee Maw a note to let her know that I'm away with the boys for a few days. Ireland here I come!!

CHAPTER EIGHT   **OFF TO THE EMERALD**

ISLE

The taxi arrives to pick me up at 4am. I need to be at the airport for 5am, as my flight is just after 6. The problem with flying to Cork is there's no direct flights from Glesga, so I need to fly doon to London and then across to Cork. A bit of a pain in the arse, but needs must. I'll still be in my B&B for 1pm.

After 2 flights and a taxi from Cork airport I arrive in Ballincollig. The taxi journey there felt like I was in another world. Lots of countryside and not as busy as Scotland. I couldn't understand a fucking word the Taxi driver said either and just kept saying,

"Aye, aye and aye."

Fuck knows what he was gibbering oan about.

Once we pass the Ballincollig sign there's a wee bit of a traffic jam. I said to the taxi driver,

"Is this normal for here?"

The place looks like it's in the middle of nowhere. His reply was along the lines of,

"No, not really, it's normally a quiet wee place."

I managed to decipher one or two of his words and came up with this.

Everybody is dressed in black and I soon cotton on that it's a funeral.

They're following a hearse to the local chapel. I get out my taxi and head to Healy's B&B. The door opens and a wee auld woman opens the door.

> "Hello der, my name is Bernadette Healy, you must be James? My husband is Dougal. He's away to a funeral at the minute, but he'll be back later for sure. Come in and make yourself at home."

> "Aye, James, eh Jamie. But my friends call me JJ."

> "No problem, James, your room is at the end of the corridor there. I'll pop the kettle on whilst you get comfortable."

I put my stuff away and head into the wee living room.

> "So, James, what brings you to Ballincollig?"

> "Well, I met a wee fella from here a couple of weeks ago in Scotland and I just wanted to pop over and visit him."

> "Ah, that's lovely son, what is his name?"

> "That's the thing. I only know his first name. James."

> "Oh, there's lots of men in this town with the name James. We have a population of just over 18,000, don't you know? What did he look like?"

I sit there drinking my coffee for the next half an hour, trying to tell auld Bernadette everything I know about auld James. Which is, basically, nothing. 18,000 folk? Aw, fur fuck sake. This isn't going to be as easy as I thought. I thought there'd be about 40 folk in this place, with two cows and a pub and every cunt would know when you've been for a shite.

I ask Bernadette to point me in the direction of the local pub. I know he likes a beer, so it's good a place as any to start my search. Two days I was planning to stay here for. Turns out, it could be longer now.

Bernadette tells me to head to Healy's Bar, in town. Healy's B&B and Healy's pub? Is every cunt here called Healy? James Healy it must be then? Case closed. If only it was that simple. I walk into Healy's bar and there's Celtic FC stuff all over the walls. I order a pint and start to blether to the auld guy behind the bar.

It turns out it's Colin Healy's grandparents that own the bar. He used to play for Celtic and Ireland. Mental. I introduce myself to his Papa. We start talking Fitba' and why I'm here etc. He tells me it's quiet in the pub at the minute as everybody is away to an auld fella's funeral. A legend in the town apparently. We chew the fat over a couple of pints and he says for me to come back later for the wake. A nice fella.

I toddle on to a few other bars but there's no sign of auld James. I have a feeling he might be at this big funeral so I decide to go on a wee pub crawl; get a bite to eat and then head back to Healy's. I've got a gut feeling, my auld pal will head back there.

It's just past 6pm now and I head towards Healy's bar. There's folk out in the street, it's that packed. Everybody is dressed in black, barring me. I stick oot like a sore thumb. I don't get to the bar without every single person saying hello to me. They all know I'm from out of town. Everybody is friendly.

It seems like the wrong place and time to ask about auld James, so I just decide to mix in with the locals, get pished and just enjoy myself. I'll start afresh in the morning and see what I can find out. I never managed to bump into auld James today, but tomorrow is a new day.

I make loads of new pals in Healy's. The craic is good and the wake goes on until about 4am. Then I stumble back to the B&B. I ask auld Bernadette to give me a shout at 9am for breakfast. This'll be fun in the morning.

Bang, bang, bang, bang!!

"Are you getting up my friend?" screams a male, Irish accent.

I look around the room and don't recognise where I am for a second. I fucking shit maself there, because I totally forgot that I was in Ireland. I put some trackies and a t-shirt on and fire through for some much needed breakfast. I've got a hangover from hell.

"Morning, James", says Bernadette. "Dougal is just finishing off your eggs. Coffee?"

"Oh, aye, please, Bernadette."

This auld fella walks through with an auld man's bunnet on. He's about 70 odd and can hardly carry my plate, the poor auld thing.

"Dougal is the name, son. I'm Bernadette's husband."

"Pleased to meet you, sir."

"I'm sorry I didn't get the chance to catch up with ye yesterday. I was at my cousin James's funeral there."

"Och, yer fine Dougal. I met up with most of the town after it yesterday at the pub."

"Oh so you were in Healy's then, my boy?"

"Erm, aye, I was. 'Til about 4am… haha."

"My nephew, Aiden, phoned at 8am and said last night you paid to go on the bus trip today, to Blarney Castle. You've to be outside Healy's at 10am."

Fuck sake, I cannae remember booking on any bus last night. I better no let them down or it might hinder my chances of finding old James. I'll ask them all questions today. Yesterday didn't seem right with them all at a wake. Today is my day. I'll be hitting them all with questions. By the end of today, I'm gonnae find old James.

I get to Healy's at 9.50am, the pub is fucking packed already. This young guy runs up to me.

"JJ! The legend. You made it!!"

Legend? Whit the fuck, man? I walk in and there's a big roar.

"JJ…JJ…JJ!!"

Holy shit man, whit did I dae last night? Every cunt in the pub shakes my hawn, then we all pile on the bus. There's beer and wine everywhere. Here we fucking go again. I think the Irish brush their teeth with alcohol…. haha.

I am handed a can of lager, so put my wee tray down. As I flip it down, the name of the bus company is there staring right at me. Healy's!! I canny believe this man. The B&B; the pub and now the bus company. I soon twig that the young guy is Aiden after a few folk shout him over. Aiden comes back to sit beside me.

"JJ, you remember Sean, Niall, Tim, Frances, Teresa, Margaret, Karen and Conor from last night don't ye?"

He's pointed to all these folk sitting round us and I'm just like,

"Ermmm.. Aye, aye, of course I do, I wasn't that drunk... haha."

Before I get steaming again, I need to start asking some questions here. My flight is booked for 2 days' time and I know absolutely nothing yet about auld James. This is gonnae be another day getting steaming, so I need some answers and, like, right now. The bus sets off and we're off to some castle. I have no idea why I agreed to it, probably pished as usual. Aye, aye, I'll go. Fud!!

"Aiden, I'm over here cause I'm trying to find an auld pal of mine and I was wondering if ye can help me, pal?"

"Of course I'll help ye, JJ. What's his name?"

"Don't laugh, but I only know his first name. James!!"

"James? Well, there's hundreds of men called James in Ballincollig, JJ, but we'll find him my Scottish pal don't you worry about that."

The singing starts and the beer is flowing. Nobody is taking this seriously. I need to find him, or I'm flinging the Bunnet in the fire at the B&B. When folk find out about this Bunnet, I'm done for.

"Are you kissing the Stone JJ?" asks Teresa.

"The Stone?" I said.

"Aye, the Blarney Stone, ya eeijit."

I haven't got a fucking clue what she's oan aboot, but say, aye, anyway.

"Good," she says. "I just hope yer not scared of heights now."

I just chuckle away as if I ken whit the fuck she's oan aboot.

The Healy's bus pulls up at the car park and we all get oot. We head towards the castle and start walking up the tiniest, narrowest stairs you've ever seen in yer life. We, eventually, get to the top and there's a queue. As I get closer I see folk starting to lie down. I'm like, whit the fuck is going on here, man?

Teresa starts to explain.

"Ok, JJ. When you get to the man on his knees there, you lie down on your back. The man holds your legs. You then hold on to the bars, hang out the edge of the castle and kiss the Blarney Stone."

"Whit the fuck, Teresa!! Hing oot the castle?"

"Yer not a chicken are ye, JJ?"

A chicken! I've seen aboot 4 wimmin and 7 guys refuse to do it so far, standing in this queue.

"Whit um a kissing it fur, does it give me a bigger wullie?"

"No, legend says, those that kiss it end up with the gift of the gab," she says.

"Right, I'm in!! C'meer you, Blarney Stone."

It's my turn. I get doon on my back, the guy hawds my pins and I hold on tae the bars. Fire myself back ootside the castle and plant the lips on the Blarney Stone. Job done!! It's a nice wee spot and after a couple of hours, a few pints and a spot of lunch, we head back to Ballincollig.

I sit beside Teresa on the way back. She's got a no' bad set of Brad Pitts on her. I'm thinking that if she plays her cards right, she might be getting a shot at the title tonight.

"Teresa, can I ask you a question?"

"Sure, what is it?"

"Was that your boyfriend I saw you in Healy's with last night?"

"My boyfriend…. haha? I don't have a boyfriend."

Sorted, she fell for the oldest trick in the book. Teresa will be getting a Scottish sausage supper the night.

"Teresa, can I ask you another question?"

"Bejasus, that Blarney Stone has definitely worked for you already. You haven't shut up since ye kissed it."

"The B&B I stay in is the Healy's, the pub we go to is Healy's and this bus company is Healy's, please tell me you have a different second name, or are you a Healy too?"

"We're all Healy's JJ, this is our annual trip to Blarney Castle."

"You're the only no- Healy on the bus... haha."

I'm starting to think I'm in the village of the fucking damned here. Healy, Healy, Healy fucking everywhere.

"Aiden says you're looking for an auld fella and that's why you're here."

"Aye that's right."

"Well, once we get back to the pub we'll be sure to start finding him for ye now."

Finally we're getting somewhere. Teresa seems like she's sober and sensible. I think she'll be the key to finding the auld yin. I've got less than 48 hours to find him now, or I might need to extend my stay. Where are ye auld boy, where are ye?

CHAPTER TEN   **NO FUCKING WAY MAN**

Oaft!! What a fucking night min. Right, where the fuck um a noo? I don't recognise the wallpaper. Who the fuck is this cuddling in? Please be a wummin, please be a wummin. Oh it's Teresa. Yuuuuuup, lovely Brad Pitts.

"Morning, Teresa!!"

"Morning, JJ. Go back to sleep will ye? We were up most of the night."

Ya dancer, she got a right good shot at the title by all accounts. I think I'll dive in for round two before I head back to the B&B.

"Would you like some breakfast before ye go on yer way, JJ?"

"I've already had some, ya sexy little minx, but, aye, I'll huv a wee bit mair, eh."

"Behave yerself man, will ye."

Teresa gets the breakfast on and I put the telly on. It's the local news and you've guessed it, it's sponsored by Healy's.

"Teresa!!"

"Yes, JJ."

"What else do the Healy's have here in Ballincollig?"

"It's not just here in Ballincollig, JJ. We started out here. We were a very poor family, until about 30 years ago when our uncle James won big at the horses. He invested it. First in the pub, then in the B&B and it snowballed from there really. We own a bank in Dublin, care homes all over Ireland, Hotels, Casino's and we own half of Dublin's plush waterfront apartment blocks. We all made a promise though that the Healy's wouldn't leave Ballincollig and we've all stuck to that. Well, barring our Colin, who made it as a professional footballer. But that's different. When Celtic come calling, you go."

"Holy Fuck Teresa. You's must be worth Millions?"

"Billions more like. Well, our uncle James was. It's a big day tomorrow for the family, his will gets read out by his Lawyer. We've had to hire the town hall there's that many of us. We're very close, so whatever we get, we get. We've never wanted for anything. Thanks to our uncle James. It's a shame you came here when you did, and not sooner."

"Why's that?"

"Well, he loved Scotland and Scottish people, he'd have loved you. He always went over four times a year to visit his old school pal, Peter."

"Aw, he sounds like he was an absolute legend of a guy, Teresa.You should be proud."

"I am proud. We all are. He always had his wee brown Bunnet on all the time, with his lucky four leaf clover embroidered on the side of it. He went over to see Pete, for the last time, a couple of weeks ago as he only had weeks to go with the cancer and wanted to see him and Scotland one last time."

"NO FUCKING WAY MAN"!!!!

"What's the matter wit ye, JJ? And don't use that disgusting language in my house man?" "Right, right, right, hawd oan a minute here. Your uncle James wore a broon Bunnet, with a four leaf clover embroidered on it?"

"Aye, that's what I said, yes."

"He went to Scotland to visit his auld pal, Pete?"

"Aye."

"What was Pete's second name, Teresa?"

"Jackson, Peter Jackson."

"This canny be happening man."

"What, JJ, what?"

"Was he a Priest, Teresa?"

"How did you know that?"

"Right, Teresa, sit doon. The man I'm looking for is your uncle James."

"He can't be JJ, yer mad."

"Teresa, Father Jackson as I knew him, was our Parish Priest. I was his altar boy and he was a family friend. He Christened m; I made my first Confession and Communion with him too. My mother told me how he appeared as the Parish Priest, years ago, and he came over from Ireland. All of his wee stories were about your uncle James and all the stuff he got up to. I feel like I've known him for years, because he's all that Father Jackson spoke about."

"Peter?"

"Aye, Peter. I was a bit down on my luck, so I went for a pint one day, about a fortnight ago and bumped into your uncle James. He gave me the best advice I've ever had and I wanted to come over here and thank him personally. But now it's too late."

"It's not too late, JJ, he's here in the local cemetery. We can go down and see him later and you can say what you have to say. When do you go home, JJ?"

"My flight is booked for tomorrow."

"Oh."

"This is all too much to take in, Teresa. Can I borrow your laptop?"

"What for, JJ?"

"I need to change my flight."

"You're leaving today?"

"No, I need to stay longer. I need to stay at least another week."

"Oh."

I extend my stay; phone my wee Maw to let her know all about the situation. She's a wee bit pissed off I said I was going away with the lads, but she forgives me. She's my Maw, after all. I ask the Healy's at the B&B if I can stay another week and they're cool too.

I need to find out more about this James Healy and how Father Jackson came to get his Bunnet. Now I know how he made his billions. But, do I tell Teresa? This is too much of a heed fuck for me the now. I say to Teresa that I'm heading back to the B&B for now and I'll catch up with her later at the pub.

Now, it's fair to say that I lived a pretty boring life, up until two weeks ago. My life revolved around losing at the bookies, losing at love and getting pished. Now I'm winning at the bookies, winning at love and still getting pished. Looks like big Meatloaf was right after all. I quite like this Teresa. A lovely lassie really, nothing like any of the lassies back home.

I head down to the pub to meet up with the Healy clan again. They're all meeting up to talk about the will at the pub. Normally I wouldn't go to anything like that, but Teresa has asked to meet up there. She said that her family all like me, so that's good. They're right up my street to be fair. Mad as a brush and like a bevvy.

I walk into Healy's and I'm greeted with my now usual call.

"JJ...JJ...JJ...!!"

Everybody shakes my hand again and make me feel very welcome.

"JJ, ya langer," is the cry from young Aiden.

Now langer, I've found out, can mean a few things and derives from the Cork area. Penis, dickhead, or an affable rogue. I hope Aiden meant the latter.

"Sit with us, my Scottish pal."

I sit beside Aiden and I scan the room looking for Teresa. There she is, standing at the bar with the other girls. Jesus, she's a beauty man.

"Can I get everybody a drink folks?"

"Aye, JJ, just tell the barmaid the same again for table seven and whatever you're having pal."

I walk up to the bar and heads towards Teresa.

"Hello gorgeous", she says.

Jesus man, I've seriously hit the jackpot here. Not only is she gorgeous, but she's seriously minted. Imagine her uncle leaves her a million plus? I order the drinks for my table and I get the ladies at the bar a drink too. I genuinely love this family, they've been nothing but kind to me since I've been here.

"Attention, attention!!,"says this big bastard at the bar. "Right folks, we all know why we're here."

I ask Aiden who the guy is and he replies,

"Me Uncle Cormac, James's only brother.

"Tomorrow our James's last Will and Testament will get read out. No matter what the outcome is, it's what he wanted so that'll be that."

"Hear, Hear..." is the cry from the Healy's.

"Let's all have a good drink tonight for our James and then we'll gather here again tomorrow night after the Town Hall and celebrate once more."

"I think I really like this family", I say to young Aiden. "Normally, in Scotland, you have a wake for somebody and that's it but you Irish take it to a different level."

"JJ, this doesn't normally happen either but James hasn't only given so much to us but to the whole of Ireland really. A lot hasn't come out about what he's done, not just for us, but for charities and such like. He really was a legend."

"I'm feeling that now Aiden, I really am, pal."

Teresa comes over and asks me if I fancy going for a walk. Fucking right I do!!

"Where you going, JJ?" Is the cry from most of the pub.

"I'll be back lads, just getting some fresh air."

Teresa eventually gets me out of there from the baying crowds, trying to give me Whiskey.

"I've got a surprise for you, JJ."

Oh ya dancer!!

She takes me down the main street and up this wee alley. I'm thinking, Teresa's wanting a shot at the title here.

"Right JJ, turn right at that gate and the first plot you come to with all the flowers and the statue of the Mother Of God, that's my uncle James's grave. You said you wanted to talk to him so go ahead. I'll wait here."

I walk up to James's grave and there it is. The big statue of Mary, the Mother of God. Here lies James Healy. 'Legend.' The Bookiebasher Of Ballincollig. 1936 - 2018. I'm stumped for words. For the first time in my life I'm actually stumped for words. What do I say to a guy who's potentially given me everything here and I don't even know him really?

"Ermmm, James, hello, JJ here. Och shut it Jamie. Right, right, sorry James. I don't know why you've done this for me, James, I really don't. I'm just a wee loser fae Scotland. I'm sorry I never gave you more time that day in the pub in Scotland. If only you'd said you were Father Jackson's pal, eh? Yer niece, Teresa, is a cracking lassie and hopefully we can continue to see each other when I go home. I don't know what to do with the Bunnet, I really don't. I was hoping for your advice, while I was here. I've heard about the stuff you've done and maybe that's what you've been trying to tell me to do also, auld pal.

"I don't want to make a decision until I've found out more about you and why you, or Father Jackson, chose me. I still don't understand why. Was it just luck, or was I meant to get that Bunnet? Anyway, James, I better shoot aff noo, I've left Teresa standing at the gate over there and it's freezing. Take care mucker."

Take care, JJ, he's deed fur fuck sake man.

"Did you talk to him" said Teresa.

"Aye,I did, I said what I needed to say, Teresa. Let's get back to the pub, beautiful."

We walk arm in arm back to Healy's. It's a lovely crisp night and it's approaching the big day. Probably the biggest Will in Irish history and the family are that down to earth that nobody outside Ireland knows about it. Tomorrow will be interesting.

CHAPTER TWELVE   THE WILL

I don't know why I got another week at the B&B, I stayed at Teresa's again last night. I wake up to the noise of the shower running in the en-suite. The good lady is soaping up those beautiful breasts, I can tell. Right, JJ, enough of that patter son. My phone goes, it's Hugo.

"JJ, where the fuck ur you man?"

"I'm in Ireland mate."

"Ireland? Whit the fuck, man?"

"It's a long story Hugo. What's up man?"

"Mel's been trying to get a hawd of you, the brewery are shutting the pub down."

"Whit the fuck, man?"

"Aye, the punters in the pub are all trying to come up with the money to buy it, they've been given a week to find it or they're selling it to that cunt Longshanks and he'll just knock it doon and build flats again."

"No fucking danger mate, that's no happening. No way"!! Give Mel ma number and get her to phone me, or get me her number. Text me it and I'll phone her, either way."

"Nae bother, mate. When you hame?"

"Next week mate, next week."

"No bother pal, Donald is keeping yer seat warm... haha."

"Fuck Donald."

"Right mate catch ye."

"Aye catch ye."

"Whit was all the swearing in here? What did I tell you about that?"

"Sorry Teresa, that was my pal from back home.They're going to shut my local pub down unless the regulars can come up with the money within a week."

"Oh no, how much is it?"

"I don't know yet. The manager will, hopefully, phone me later."

"Oh, ok."

"Right, I need to go soon, JJ. We're all meeting at the pub and then heading to the Town Hall. I'm sorry, you can't come to this today."

"No, no, don't be silly, it's fine. I've got this pub thing to sort out anyway. I'll get a shower and head back to the B&B."

We both get dressed and go our separate ways. Teresa to the Town Hall to meet the Healy's and I'm off to the Electrical shop to get a laptop, I have a plan.

I get back to the B&B with my new laptop, it takes about 20 minutes to set it all up and I'm in. Straight to Google!! James Healy, Ballincollig. Enter!!

LOCAL MAN WINS MILLIONS AT THE RACES

THE BOOKIE-BASHER OF BALLINCOLLIG STRIKES AGAIN.

He's everywhere man. I read as much as I can about him. I click on the images and there he is with the brown Bunnet on. Incredible.

My phone rings; it's a number I don't recognise, but it's a local one from back home. I better answer it.

"Hello...Hello,, JJ is that you? It's Mel."

"Aye, Hugo telt me all about it."

"We're fucked JJ, we're really fucked."

"How much do they want Mel?"

"£180,000 for the pub and £220,000 for the 5 bedroom apartment upstairs. They want £400,000 in total by the end of the week, or they're selling it to Longshanks, who has the money waiting. "They promised me first refusal if they were ever selling it and we've tried, but we canny even muster £10,000 between us all. It's just not fair, JJ."

Mel starts greeting doon the phone.

"Right, Mel, pack that shite in. Send me the brewery's bank details and I'll see what I can do pal."

"Where are you gonnae get £400k from, ya daft bastard?"

"I don't know Mel, but I'll try pal."

How the fuck am I gonna get £400,000, man? I cannae gamble here 'cause if anybody sees me with James's Bunnet on I'll get murdered and I'll lose Teresa too. What do I fucking do, man? Go hame and save the pub or stay here with Teresa and the Healy's? Aw fuck my life man. I decide to sleep on it for a couple of hours. Teresa has been riding me like Seabiscuit, man, I'm fucked, proper fucked.

I wake up to my phone going off again. Mr fucking popular the day. It's Teresa,

"Right, we're done."

"Whit do you mean we're done, Teresa? I really like you."

"No, ya eeijit. We're done at the Town Hall."

"Oh sorry, darling, I've just woke up, doesn't matter. I thought you meant we're done."

"Get me at Healy's, JJ."

I get a shower, get my threads on and get down to Healy's to hear Teresa's news. I walk in and the whole family are there.

"So, how'd it go Teresa?"

"'Mon outside, JJ, I can't hear myself think in here."

Teresa has got a white envelope in her hand and I'm thinking, she's waited to open it in front of me. Awwwwww.

"Ok, we all got 2 million Euros each. The 46 of us, and a monthly allowance of 10,000 Euros each for life. All the property went to his brother, Cormac, and that's it. Well, excluding one last thing."

"That's it?"

"Aye, JJ, that's it."

"I thought you were going to open your envelope in front of me there... haha.

"It's not my envelope, JJ, it's yours."

"Awwww, you've got me a wee present babes?"

"It's not from me, it's from James. My Uncle Cormac wants to speak to you, JJ, two minutes. Don't open it just yet."

Teresa heads back into the pub and out comes this massive guy Cormac, James's brother. I'm thinking, don't fucking eat me big man.

"Cormac", he holds his shovel like hand out.

"Eh James, I mean Jamie, I mean, JJ, sir."

"Now, this has come as a bit of a surprise to me and you've saved me a journey really. My brother's dying wish was for everything to get squared away properly and that included you getting this letter. He told me your daily routine, the pub you drank in, the bookies you lived in and also your other haunts, so I knew you'd be easy to find.

"He requested that you, and only you, reads this letter and then destroy it. He told me that he met you in Scotland and gave you a gift, that was all he told me. Once he died, I was to deliver this letter to you. You're here now, so read it out here by yourself and then come inside and throw it in the fire when you're done."

I wasn't gonnae argue with the big cunt or he'd fling me in the fire.

Do I read it or do I pretend I've read it and just fling it in the fire? Do I also go back to the B&B and fling that fucking Bunnet in the fire tae? I'm shaking, this is all getting a bit too much.

CHAPTER THIRTEEN   **THE LETTER**

Here goes nothing, I take a look around and there's nobody in sight. I heard Cormac tell everybody to stay inside for ten minutes and he bolted the pub door shut. This is it, the truth, the moment I've been waiting for. Fuck it, I open it. You only live once!!

Dear JJ,

When I met you, I only had up to a month to live. I expect if I made it that long, it's been quite a whirlwind month for you and you've realised that you have a very lucky Bunnet on your hands? I trust my brother Cormac has handed this to you and the envelope hasn't been tampered with in any way?

There are only four people who know about the powers of the Bunnet. One of them is alive and the other three are deceased. So once you've read this letter then please destroy it immediately. You'll be wondering why you've been chosen, eh? Well here's why, my boy.

You met me, and you've met Cormac, but there's one other brother. My Mother had him out of wedlock so as you may or may not know, that was a big no, no years ago. My Mother had to give him up for adoption. His name was Peter. She had two daughters as well, Mairead and Karen.

We never knew about Peter until my Mother was dying and she told us about him on her death bed. It turns out that my best pal from the estate in Ballincollig was actually my big brother.

Once the news got out when Peter got to around 40, he couldn't take it and fled the village to join the Priesthood. He ended up in Scotland. We kept in touch and I visited him four times a year. I begged him and begged him to come home but he couldn't face the shame. He did nothing wrong and had nothing to be ashamed of.

Every time I came over, I attended his masses. It was quite funny when he told his stories half way through the mass and they were about me. I used to see you when you were a wee altar boy and spoke to your mum, Terry, after most of the services.

I could see the struggle that your Mum was going through trying to bring you up on her own. I offered to help her many, many times but she refused. She'd tell me that she worked full time in the textiles factory and if that's what God wanted for her, then so be it.

I bought the textiles factory and she never knew. A guy called Longshanks wanted to buy it 20 years ago and turn the area into flats. I stepped in at the last minute and offered more money so your mum wouldn't lose her job.

Every time I came back, my feelings grew stronger and stronger for your mother, but her only love was you and that's what she lived for. I watched you when I came for my visits to Scotland. I'd see you stumble about in the pub, go from the pub to the bookies and so on.

I'm giving you the chance that I had, don't fuck it up!!

The Bunnet got handed down to me by an old Irish guy named Seamus. He used it just to feed his family by gambling in cockfighting. He'd go down to the Blackpitts in the South of Dublin, gamble on the cockfighting then return home to feed his family for the year.

This is all up to you now, JJ. Peter knew about the Bunnet because, as you heard in his stories at Mass, he enjoyed the fruits of it too. He was my best pal, my brother in the end.

I put the Bunnet in his box that was going to the Charity shop when I was clearing out his flat and I led you to it, with that chat in the pub that day. I knew it fitted you 'cause you stole it off me in the pub one day, pished, and tried it on. It fitted you perfectly.

I don't know what else to say JJ, I loved your mother. That's why I never ever married. Look after her for me son and look after yourself. The Bunnet is now yours, do the right things with it, JJ.

Yours Faithfully

James Healy

Well fuck me sideways!! Oaft!! Where do you fucking start with that wan? My heed is fried, completely fried. I better go back into the pub, fling this in the fire and try and act normal here. Holy fuck!!

I walk in,

    "JJ...JJ...JJ...!!"

They never fail.... haha. What a family!! I'm going to miss them all when I go back to Scotland. What do I tell Teresa and how do I leave her? I've really fallen for her. I take one last look at the envelope, give it a kiss and fling into the roaring fire in the pub.

"JJ, will ye come over here?" says this stunning looking woman in her 50's.

"Errrrr, hello there."

"Aren't you going to say hello to Teresa's mum? I'm Mairead."

"Oh, hello Mairead, Teresa has told me all about ye."

"All good I hope, JJ?"

"Aye, errr, all good."

"Teresa, I need to go."

"Go where, JJ?"

"Back to the B&B. I've got a splitting sore headache and won't be much company tonight. I'll catch up with you in the morning ok? I'll take you for breakfast."

I sneak out the pub somehow and head back to the B&B. That letter has freaked me out.

I get back to the room and get the Bunnet out. I just stare at it for an hour and don't say a word. What am I going to do? There isn't a person in the world who wouldn't want to be in my position right now, but I don't know if I can take the responsibility.

I wake up at 8am with my phone ringing, it's Teresa.

"Hullo," in my sleepy daze.

"I thought you were taking me for breakfast Mr? Get up, get in a shower and I'll meet you in town at 9."

"Ok boss."

I follow the good lady's orders and duly meet her in town, bang on 9am.

"You feeling better today JJ."

"I am, so aye. Just needed a good night's sleep there. Yesterday was a lot to take in with the pub shutting, your uncle's will etc etc."

"Och the pub will be fine, somebody will buy it, JJ."

"Aye, Longshanks will buy it ,the bastard."

"JJ!! Language!!"

"Och, sorry Teresa, but he is a bastard."

She gives me the evils.

"You've got some washing at mine, do you want to come round and get it after this?"

"Aye of course, I need to start packing my stuff to go hame."

"When are you going hame, JJ?"

"Not tomorrow, but the next day, Teresa"

"Oh, ok then."

She's went from all smiley to looking heartbroken, to be honest.

We finish breakfast and head back to hers. All my washing is neatly washed and folded in a clear white bag and there's some money and paper on top of it.

"What's all that on top Teresa?"

"That's what was in your pockets, 267 Euro's and 40 cents and a few receipts. Oh, and a bit of paper that looks like bank account details, so I thought you'd want to keep that too?"

"Och, no, just fling that in the bin, that's the account details of the brewery for the pub. No way I'm raising the money so that's that."

"Ok, I'll fling that and the receipts in the bin."

"The money Teresa, just keep a hawd of that, I want to put 500 Euro's behind the bar tomorrow night since it's my last night here to thank everyone for being so nice."

"Och, don't be so silly, JJ."

This might sound weird but I don't want to go home. I love it here I really do. What have I honestly got to go back for? To sit in a bookies and a pub all day listening to Donald talking pish? Ok, I'll miss my pal Hugo, Alberto is alright too, oh, and Mel from the pub. My wee Maw tae, I suppose. Snap oot of it JJ, ye don't belong here, ye belong in Scotland son.

Teresa says she's a wee bit tired after that breakfast and fancies a wee nap and do I want to come? Come, ye say hen? Fucking right I dae, pal. We head up to bed for a.... aherm... snooze....

After our, snooze. I'm lying there spooning Teresa thinking I'm the luckiest guy on the planet. She's absolutely stunning. I'm playing with her jet black hair and kissing her neck, she smells amazing too. I don't want to leave her but know that I have to. We spend the rest of the day and night in bed. The perfect way to spend my second last day in Ireland.

It's approaching midnight, we've been watching movies all day and laughing with each other. Kissing, cuddling and just enjoying each other. She looks at me and says,

> "So, tomorrow is our last full day together, eh?"

> "I don't want to think about it Teresa, I really don't."

> "Why, JJ?" she giggles.

> "Teresa, I love you"!!

Right, hawd the fucking bus here. I've never said that to anybody in my life before. Where did that come from JJ? Oh Jesus, oh Jesus, you've fucked it now mate.

> "JJ."

"Yes, Teresa. I love you too."

"Really?"

"Yes, really."

We don't say another word, just smile at each other, kiss and cuddle a little more then fall asleep. A perfect end to a perfect day.

I wake up in the middle of the night having a panic attack. I think I've ran out of money somehow, so take my phone to the toilet and check my online banking. The banking is app is down because they're working on the site until 6am. Fur fuck's sake, man. I go into the kitchen and try to work it all oot. It's my last full day here today and want to make it a good one for Teresa and all the Healy's.

I mind I put £4000 in last week, then around £3000 after that. Maybe a wee bit more. I've spent £500 on flights, £600 on the B&B even though I think I've only slept there twice. I've spent close to £3000 on food and drink since I've been here, buying every cunt drink. Right, I can go back to sleep now. I've got enough for tomorrow until I get hame.

I'm lying there next to the most beautiful woman on the planet, I've got plenty money left to have a good send off with the Healy's and I've still got my Bunnet back at the B&B. I'm one lucky boy.

I waken up bright as a button. I start sending all the Healy's a text. 6pm tonight in Healy's, JJ's leaving do!! As the morning goes on, one by one they all get back to me. Healy's will be rammed tonight. I go into the kitchen and start to make the beautiful Teresa breakfast in bed.

I decide to go back to the B&B and get most of my stuff. Teresa wants me to stay with her tonight as it'll be our last ever night together. I pick up everything really, barring the Bunnet and a couple of Jackets. I get my passport and my boarding pass as well and put it all in my suitcase then head back to Teresa's.

It'll make it easier in the morning saying goodbye to Bernadette and Dougal. I can just swing by in the morning in the taxi and pick up my last bits. I'll probably be too hungover in the morning to pack so best to do it all now.

I still can't bring myself to tell her about the Bunnet, but I've promised myself I will before I go. I can't bring it to hers either as it'll ruin everything if she just finds it and I haven't told her. I'll tell her before I leave for the airport tomorrow morning.

I take Teresa out for lunch and we do a bit of clothes shopping for tonight's leaving do. We'll both be looking the part. We get home to Teresa's, she models her new stuff and I model mine. Sorted!! She runs a bubble bath, pours us both a glass of wine and we hop in.

I'm happy about going home now, but tomorrow is the deadline for the pub, so I'm a wee bit nervous about that. Longshanks has won by the looks of it. Our little community will never be the same again. Bastard!!

While I'm in the bath with Teresa, my mobile goes aff three or four times.

"Go and answer it", says Teresa.

"Naw, they can wait, I'd rather be here with you."

After topping the hot water up two or three times, we're both like prunes so decide to get oot the bath. I check my phone. Two missed calls from Mel and two from Hugo. I better phone them, Hugo first.

"Hugo!!"

"JJ, have you spoke to Mel yet?"

"Naw, why?"

"Jist phone her pal, it's better coming fae her mate."

"Ok pal, I will do. Talk to ye later bud."

"Aye."

I'm shaking like a shitting dug here, what can it be?

"Mel."

"JJ, is that you?"

"Aye, whit is it? Hit me with it."

"We have a new buyer for the pub!!!"

"Whit?"

"Somebody has made the £400,000 bid before the week deadline and the brewery have accepted it."

"Woah, woah, woah, Mel. This doesn't make sense, pal."

"Somebody has paid it. It must be one of the punters. It's only us that knew about the first refusal and the brewery have accepted it. They want to remain anonymous. The pub shuts on Monday for a full refurb and a new name unveil, eight weeks later, it's a done deal."

"Ya FUCKING beauty!! Sorry, Teresa."

"Who's Teresa, JJ?"

"Och it doesn't matter the now. That's unbelievable news to come home to."

"One last thing, JJ, the new owner wants to keep the same staff in the same positions too, so I won't lose my job either and with a pay rise also."

"Och, that's brilliant Mel, I'm really chuffed pal, I really am. I'll see ye the morra. Need to shoot pal. Bye."

What a last day in Ireland this is turning out to be. Spent the day with the lovely Teresa; good news from home and now to party with the Healy's. I'm going to enjoy tonight now without a care in the world. I'm going to miss this place dearly.

The taxi arrives at 5.45pm to pick myself and Teresa up. She's looking amazing in her red dress and red shoes, with bright Red lipstick on. I've got my Blue suit on, nice crisp white shirt and Brown shoes. Looking dapper too. We arrive at Healy's expecting it to be quiet. It's anything but.

"JJ... JJ... JJ...!!"

My usual greeting from the Healy's and they're all there. Even Bernadette and Dougal are there from the B&B to see me off. I go over to them straight away, as I've hardly see them all week, thanks to the lovely Teresa.

"Hi, folks. Sorry for being your worst guest ever."

"You're fine son, enjoy yourself, life is too short", says Dougal.

The party gets in to full swing and the whiskey, beer and the songs are in full flow. Mairead keeps telling me how much Teresa is going to miss me and as the time is ticking away, my guts are turning at the thought of leaving her.

Just as everybody is having a laugh and a good drink, the pub doors burst open and four Gardai officers storm in. The barman stops the music.

"Are Bernadette and Dougal here?" says the first officer first through the door.

"Aye," shouts Dougal from the back of the room.

"Can you come with us, sir?"

"Of course," says Dougal, with Bernadette right beside him.

Everyone is looking out the window in bemusement and then Bernadette suddenly sinks to her knees and starts screaming and crying. Everyone rushes out the pub.

"It's gone, it's gone!!" screams Dougal.

"What's gone?" asks Cormac.

"The B&B, it's gone, Cormac."

"What do you mean, it's gone?"

The Gardai officer gathers everyone round and explains.

"About two hours ago, Healy's B&B went on fire. By the time we could get fire engines in from Cork, the fire was that fierce that it burned the whole B&B to the ground. There was nothing we could do."

There's a look of shock on everyone's face.

The mood has gone from a massive high, to an all-time low. The family are devastated!! I start to console Teresa and Mairead. Everybody is in bits and we do our best to comfort the most distressed ones. The Bunnet has gone also, but to be honest, I'm more concerned about Bernadette and Dougal right now. The party finishes and everybody goes home. Cormac takes Bernadette and Dougal back to his place and I head back to Teresa's.

We get back to Teresa's and she asks me what I had in the B&B. I told her that luckily I only left a couple of jackets there. The rest of my stuff was in my suitcase in her hallway. She asks me about my Passport and boarding pass etc. and luckily, again, I packed it all.

I've lost the Bunnet and now it's all starting to sink in. I'm going back to Scotland tomorrow without the Bunnet and I'm going back without Teresa. Just when things were looking up for me, I'm brought back down to fucking reality. I'm going back to Scotland with nothing.

I hardly slept a wink last night thinking about Bernadette and Dougal. 70 years' worth of possessions, all up in smoke and gone forever. The only comforting thing is, I know they have an amazing family to look after them. I can hear Teresa cooking me breakfast already. This is going to be one emotional day.

"Morning, Teresa."

"Morning, JJ. Coffee?"

"Oh, yes please gorgeous."

I can't take my eyes off her this morning. I want to savour every last second of this before the taxi comes.

"Right, ye sure ye have everything for this flight now?"

"Aye I'm sorted."

"Good."

The taxi is due in ten minutes. I'm dressed and good to go and I sit Teresa down on the bed for my departing words.

"Teresa, what's meant to be, is meant to be in life my love."

"Do I think this will be the last time we ever see each other?"

"Not a chance!!"This isn't some holiday romance, let me tell you. I love you Teresa Healy. I loved you from the moment I first saw you. I'm just over the water and when I get my life sorted out over there, then I want you to join me. Don't cry Teresa, I'm not worth the tears. I'm just a scumbag, no user from the West Coast of Scotland."

"No, yer not, JJ, yer amazing."

"No you're amazing Teresa and so is your family. You have all taught me so much this week and I'm devastated to be leaving you all, I really am."

"Well, don't then JJ."

"I have to, for now Teresa. I can't just give up my life in Scotland right now. I promise we'll be together, Teresa, I promise."

"We better be, JJ, I love you too."

Beep ...Beep!! The taxi arrives. Myself and Teresa have one last kiss and cuddle at the door and I don't turn around cause I'm greeting my eyes out and I don't want her to see. I'm thinking about everything on the way to the airport. Teresa; the Bunnet, the B&B, the pub back home and the Healy's. It's been a whirlwind few weeks but it isn't over yet.

I pull up in the Taxi outside my Maw's just before 7pm, two planes and two taxis later. Shattered. I open the front door to be greeted by her voice.

"I'm in the kitchen. Who's that?"

"It's me Maw, JJ."

She comes out the kitchen, wraps her arms around me and gives me a big kiss.

"Where have you been aw this time, ya dafty?"

I tell her to grab a bottle of wine. We both head to the Living room and I spend the next 3 hours telling her everything. Well everything except the Bunnet. I've decided to leave the Bunnet where it belongs. In the ashes. I didn't have it in me to keep it anyway and it wouldn't have been long before it got exposed. I'm not a clever person, especially when I'm drunk and after a few Beers, I would've either lost it or gave it away no doubt.

After our chat I head up the stairs to my bedroom. I've got £31 left in my bank account after my trip to Ireland. I get my Giro money tomorrow, so I'm back to fucking square one. I canny wait to see the boys tomorrow and Mel in the pub. I'm lying in bed and know that I'd rather be in Ireland with Teresa.

I've got some serious life decisions to make soon but without the Bunnet, I have no way of making money now. The only jobs about here are in the textile factory and there's no way they'll take me back on. I want to be with Teresa but don't want her to think I'm just after her money. My life is fucked again, I need some fucking luck once again.

I'm awakened at 6.25am by the front door slamming. That's my wee Maw away to work again. She does 7am - 5pm, Monday to Friday and never complains once. She just gets on with life and doesn't bother a soul. I send Teresa a wee text telling her that I love her and I miss her. I might as well get oot my Maggie Thatcher.

I fire doon to Sammy's shop for some rolls.

>"Top of the morning tae ye, JJ" he says. "I hear yer Irish now?"

>"Naw, I'm no' Sammy. Two Rolls and a Racing Post please."

>"What's this you were in Ireland, the prostitutes better over there?"

>"I've never been with a prostitute in my life, Sammy, so bolt man."

The guy's a complete throbber man, but it's the only shop aboot here.

My phone starts going, it's my wee Maw.

>"Hello Maw. Whit? ...Yer breaking up. Right, I'll see ye at the hoose."

I get back to the hoose and my Maw is already there.

>"JJ, apparently the silent owner of the Textile Factory has died and we've all been sent home on full pay for the week. We've all to turn up on Friday at 9am to meet the new owner."

>"Oh, right Maw...That's... ermm bad news about the owner but good news you have a new one. Maybe I can get a job noo, with a new owner coming in?"

"Probably no', JJ, it's still the same Supervisors."

"Oh, aye, so it is, that's me fucked then."

I leave my wee Maw efter breakfast and head doon to the bookies.

"JJ yer back!!" says Hugo.

"Aye, mate, I've missed ye man. Whit's been happening?"

"Och, the usual mate, fuckall."

We chew the fat and I tell him about my trip and about Teresa etc. All that chatter has made me thirsty so I head over to the pub for a pint.

"JJ, yer back pal?"

"Aye Mel, jist thought I'd pop in and see ye afore the pub shuts for eight weeks as well."

"Did ye hear about the textile factory, JJ?"

"Aye, my Maw just telt me."

"Poor wee owner died eh, efter saving it fae that bastard Longshanks all those years ago."

"Aye, some man he was, I heard."

"Eh?"

"Aw, nothing, Mel."

There's five auld Men in the pub but there's one guy sitting in the corner, with a Bunnet oan, reading a paper and I cannae see his face but, he's some size of man. I just go back to telling Mel all about my trip to Ireland. After a few minutes I get a tap on the shooder.

"JJ, my boy," in an Irish accent.

The cunt nearly broke my shooder. I turn roon,

"Cormac!! What are you doing here?"

"I came to see you."

"Eh?"

"Come over here and sit, I have some paperwork for you to sign."

"Paperwork to sign?"

Cormac gets us baith a pint and a Whisky and we head for the corner of the pub. He comes right out with it.

"How would you like to be the new owner of the textile factory?"

"Eh?"

"I'm offering it to you JJ for free, no catches."

"I'm not following you here Cormac."

"James told me about your mother and how she was his only true love in life. He'd want me to do this. We'll make you the new silent owner. Just sign here and it's yours. We'll go to the bank today and I'll deposit a Million Pounds into a business account for you and you just take a wage each month and carry on as normal."

This isn't happening here. I woke up this morning with 30 quid and now I could own the place I cannae even get a joab in. I could own it in the next two minutes.

"Cormac, I don't know what to say."

"Say nothing son, just sign here and I'll sort everything out with the lawyers."

I sign all the paperwork and it's done. I own the fucking textile factory.

Madness!!

> "Teresa is asking for you son, she's been round at our Mairead's breaking her heart since you left. Once all this textile factory business is all sorted out, get your arse over to Ballincollig and see her."

> "I will Cormac, I will."

> "Right JJ, I'll go and sort all this out. My Lawyer will be in touch."

> "See ya Cormac and thanks once again."

> "Don't thank me son, thank your Mother and James."

Talk about life being a rollercoaster and you've just got to ride it. Holy shitballs!! What the fuck do I do now? Tell my Maw? Naw, but I'm definitely gonna surprise her that's for sure.

I finish my pint and my whisky and just head up the road. My heid is all over the place again, so I give the bookies a miss. I walk in and my wee Maw is greeting.

> "Wits the matter maw?"

> "Whit if that bastard Longshanks has bought it and he turns it into flats son?"

> "He won't get it Maw, don't worry."

> "He will, he will, there's naebody else aboot here wi' money, JJ."

> "Wait till Friday, I'm sure everything will be fine."

My phone goes and it's a text from Teresa.

Congratulations Mr.Textile Factory Owner!!

Love and miss you loads big boy!!

Teresa xxx

Cormac must've told her already. At least that's cheered her up. I'm missing her like fuck, I need to see her. I decide to Facetime her to at least get a swatch of the Brad Pitts.

> "Hiya gorgeous"!!
>
> "Hiya, JJ!! I take it Cormac told you the news?"
>
> "He did that, aye. He got the first boat over this morning to come and tell you face to face. We all thought it was a brilliant idea."
>
> "Well I can' believe the gesture to be fair."
>
> "Well, JJ, we all love you over here, so it gets you and your wee mammy set up for life now. We just need to work out something now."
>
> "Aye we do that, we do that."

We talk for over an hour on Facetime but I don't get a swatch of the Brad Pitts. She's no' that type of lassie. We make plans and she even booked a flight to come over in eight weeks' time. I can even afford my own place now, once all the money gets transferred and I get my own salary.

I've got eight weeks now to sort my life out. She planned the trip so she can see the new pub when it opens as well. I've told the whole toon about her now and everybody cannae wait to meet her, especially my wee Mum. Speaking of my Mum, I'm just about to turn her wee world upside down.

My Maw has worked in that textiles factory for 32 years and she hasn't even made it to Supervisor. She knows that place inside out and better than anybody. She doesn't know it yet, but she's got a wee surprise coming for her in the post tomorrow morning.

"Aw, JJ, I'm shitting maself for tomorrow morning son."

"Why maw?"

"It's the big reveal, the new owner."

"Och, I telt you it'd be fine Maw don't worry."

We have a wee bit of tea and toast and we both get off to our beds for her big day tomorrow.

"Maw ye up?"

"Aye son."

It's 6.45pm and I decide to make my Maw breakfast for a change. She comes into the kitchen just after 7 and I hear the letterbox going.

"That must be the Postman maw, want to get the letters while I pour the coffee's?"

She walks in with one big brown envelope.

"Who's that fur Maw?"

"Me, son."

"Oh, ok."

She opens it and starts reading it. I can see her eyes welling up and then she just bursts oot greeting.

"Maw, whit's the matter?"

"Read this, JJ, read it"!!

Dear Miss Johnson,

               I'd just like to introduce myself, I'm the owner of JJ International LTD and have recently purchased the Textiles Factory. I have been following the business very closely over recent years and in light of all your hard work, loyalty and 32 years' service to the factory, I'd like to promote you from shop floor worker to Chief Exectutive. You will be representing JJ International LTD as our spokesperson as the new owner would like to remain, like the previous owner, a silent one as well. Your salary will go from £13.326 per annum to £125,000 per annum

I hope this is a sufficient salary for your new role? As Chief Executive of the Company, your first role will be to chair the meeting today at the Factory and explain to everybody the following changes......

The letter went on and on and on about a pay-rise for the shop floor workers. Promotions for some of my Maw's pals and I also got rid of some dead wood. Her wee face was a picture it really was. I've never seen her so happy, bless her.

Seven weeks pass and at the textiles factory, business is booming. My wee Maw has settled into her role perfectly and she's employed Bonnie as her PA. Bonnie might love the boaby but she's a whizz roon a computer. Everything is going great and next week my darling arrives for a few days.

I've managed to rent a nice hoose on a year's lease, until I buy something and I've just been putting the final lick of paint on it for Teresa's arrival. Talking about paint, the new pub is coming along beautifully. It's all clean and fresh and the toon can't wait for the grand opening next week.

Everything seems to be ready except the sign on the front. Nobody knows who the new owner, or owners, are. It's the closest guarded secret in the toon since the Bunnet was around. I got a sneak peek inside from Mel, but they're leaving the sign until an hour before opening. Nobody has a clue, but Mel's still running it, so that'll do for everybody.

Today is the day!! Teresa arrives so I make my way to the airport. The Arrivals gate opens and there she is. My beautiful, Irish girlfriend, looking as gorgeous as ever. We kiss and cuddle and squeeze the life out of each other. I can't wait 'til everybody meets her. The pub grand opening isn't until tomorrow so everybody is going to meet her there.

We head back to my rented place. I gave my Maw a set of keys, so she's there on our arrival. We pull up at the house, the smell of fresh paint stings the air.

"Oh you've decorated for me have you now?"

Oh how I've missed that sexy Irish accent.

"Yes, dear."

We go inside and my Maw has the biggest smile on her face.

"You must be Teresa? Awww look at ye. Gorgeous."

"Aw, thanks Miss Johnson."

"You can call me Terry darling. You look beaming lass, so you do."

"Awwww, thanks."

I get Teresa up the stairs with all her stuff whilst Mum puts the kettle on. We order in a Chinese and chat the night away. Tomorrow is the big day for the town. At 12, mid-day, we find out the new owner or owners of the pub and this wee town can get back to normal.

CHAPTER NINETEEN   FAMILY

The big day for town finally arrives. After breakfast we head down the main street for a walk and the town is busy. The balloons are all tied outside the pub and the ribbon is across the doorway. Mel is ootside brushing the last bits and bobs away from the front door.

"I'm liking the green everywhere Mel, even a Green ribbon... haha," I shout.

"Aye, I think Kermit the Frog has bought it."

Me and Teresa just laugh.

We head back to the house and I see Teresa get a white envelope out of her suitcase.

"What's that for darling?"

"A wee surprise for you, JJ."

"Awww, thanks."

"You're not getting it now, I'll give you it at the pub."

"What is it? The deeds for the pub... haha?"

"Not likely, better than that."

"Eh?"

We head down to the pub and the new sign is up but it's covered. There's a guy there in a suit, nobody recognises him. He must be the new owner. We see him ask a few folk for Mel and then he eventually talks to her. He gets on to the platform with Mel and gets ready to give his speech.

Teresa turns to me and hands me the White envelope. Surely not? I open the envelope and it's a Hospital scan picture.

"Congratulations, JJ, you're going to be a Daddy, I'm 9 weeks pregnant."

"What the fuck?"

Mel is instructed to hand out beers and whisky to the gathered crowd by this guy on the stage. Everybody has a glass.

"I don't know what to say, Teresa, I really don't."

"Well you'd better say something, JJ."

"Ermmm….. ermmmm."

The guy starts speaking and my mouth is on the floor. He's Irish.

"Ladies and Gentleman. I'm a spokesperson for the new owners of the pub. It gives me great pleasure to welcome onto the stage, Teresa and James."

"Eh?"

Teresa starts smiling and she takes my hand and we walk towards the stage. My Maw, Mel, Hugo and every cunt else in the toon is as much in disbelief about this as I am. We walk onto the stage and she pulls the cord for the sign. "

"Welcome to Healy's," she shouts into the mic.

There it is!! The big fuck-off Healy's sign, right in front of the pub.

Everybody is going bananas and cuddling each other.

"Well done JJ, ye kept that quiet son," shouts Hugo.

I'm fucking stunned; how did she manage to pull this off? She's looking at me, smiling, I pass the white envelope to my Maw. She opens it and bursts oot greeting.

"I'm gonnae be a Granny, everybody"!!

Teresa looks at me and whispers in my ear,

"Everything comes in 3's."

I look at her and go,

"Naw, fuck naw, wit noo."

Beeeeeep, beeeeeep..... I turn roon and there's a bus coming up the main street. A fucking Healy's bus!! They're all here!! They all pile aff the bus, every single one of them.

Bernadette, Dougal, Aiden, Cormac and Mairead get off first.

"Mum this is Mairead, she's going to be a Granny too."

We all just burst into tears. What a surprise and what a day!!

"I'm going to be a Daddy, everybody" I scream into the mic.

"JJ... JJ... JJ...!!"

We drink into the wee small hours – well, except for the pregnant Lady of course. It's great to see all the Healy's again. I'm bowled over with what's happened recently. There's two more things though that I need to do now.

"Night, Mel."

"Night, JJ, ermm.. I mean boss."

"Less of that pish, JJ, to you pal."

I tell Teresa that she's changed my life in the past 24 hours and now I want to change hers.

"How can you possibly do that, JJ?"

"You'll see."

We walk along the main street and turn right up Sweets Way to the local cemetery. She looks at me all confused and I say,

"Do you trust me?"

"Of course I trust you, JJ."

"Well then, come with me."

I take her inside and put a light on using my phone.

"What are we doing here JJ?"

"You'll see."

"Here lies Father Peter Jackson" I say.

"Ah, is this uncle James's friend, J?."

"It's not Uncle James's friend Teresa, it's your uncle James's brother."

"I don't follow" she says.

"Your Granny had Peter out of wedlock and was forced to give him up Teresa, he's your Mum's big brother, your uncle. If it wasn't for your Uncle Peter, we would've never met. Your uncle James knew he was his biological brother, but not until your Gran was on her death bed. It all came out then. Before James died on his last visit to Scotland, he gave me his Bunnet. I'll explain about the Bunnet in the morning, that's another story.

"Teresa what I'm trying to say is that all of this started with Peter Jackson and the Bunnet so this is where it's going to end. I know today has been one big shock to the both of us, but it doesn't end there."

"What are you going on about now, JJ?"

"I don't have a ring just yet, but it seems like the perfect time and place."

JJ gets down on one knee in front of Father Jackson's grave.

"We're going to have a child together and we have a business together now. Teresa, will you marry me?"

"Awww, JJ, of course I will.

THE END

Story by Scott Alcroft

Printed in Great Britain
by Amazon